Old Tom
Man of Mystery

Leigh HOBBS

PEACHTREE
ATLANTA

Angela Throgmorton was exhausted.
The time had come to make a few changes.

Old Tom had been a beautiful baby.
But now he was big enough to help with the housework.

So Angela made a list of things for him to do.

She knew that it might not be easy to get Old Tom to help.

But Angela wasn't one to give up.
"Where would you like to start?" she asked nicely.

Suddenly, Old Tom felt sick.

So Angela gave him a kiss and put him to bed.
"Now lie still and be a good boy," she said. "You'll soon be well enough to help."
But Old Tom had other ideas.

While Angela was busy dusting and wiping and scrubbing and sweeping…

Old Tom was busy too.
He had changed into…the Man of Mystery!

Angela baked some cakes for when Old Tom got better.

Suddenly she noticed fresh fur on her clean floor.

Then Angela heard a noise in the next room.

There were crumbs on the carpet!

"Where could *they* have come from?" she wondered.

Angela paid a surprise visit to Old Tom, with a card and some flowers.

"I do hope you'll be better soon," she said.
"And then you can help around the house."

Angela was tired and went to bed early—
only to be woken by mysterious footsteps.

Angela followed the footsteps through the house,

and out the window.

The Man of Mystery ran off into the night

and so did Angela Throgmorton.

The Man of Mystery said hello to the neighbors.

And to their children too.

The Man of Mystery stopped for a late-night snack.

Suddenly he remembered the list of things to do at home.

The Man of Mystery paused at a restaurant.
His manners looked strangely familiar.

Lots of things about this
Man of Mystery were familiar.

Who could it be?

Angela thought she knew.

She hurried home.

And as she expected, *someone* wasn't in his room.

When Old Tom arrived home late, Angela was waiting.

"So, too sick to help!" snapped Angela Throgmorton.
Old Tom was sent straight to bed.

But Angela couldn't stay cross for long. In the morning the Man of Mystery got a big breakfast in bed. After all, he would be needing his strength. There was still that long, long list of things for him to do around the house.

For Ann Haddon (Jess)
and Ali Lavau

Ω

Published by
PEACHTREE PUBLISHERS
1700 Chattahoochee Avenue
Atlanta, Georgia 30318-2112
www.peachtree-online.com

ISBN 1-56145-346-3

10 9 8 7 6 5 4 3 2 1
First Edition

Illustrations created in pen, ink, gouache, and acrylic.

Printed in China

Library of Congress Cataloging-in-Publication Data

Hobbs, Leigh.
Old Tom, Man of Mystery / Leigh Hobbs.-- 1st ed.
    p. cm.
Originally published: Australia : Little Hare Books, 2003.
Summary: When Angela Throgmorton decides that Old Tom is now big enough
to help around the house, he has other ideas.
ISBN 1-56145-346-3
[1. Housekeeping--Fiction. 2. Helpfulness--Fiction. 3. Cats--Fiction.] I. Title.

PZ7.H65236Ojy 2005
[Fic]--dc22
                              2005000771